Percy
and the
Pirates

Russell Punter

Illustrated by Kate Sheppard

Reading Consultant: Alison Kelly
Roehampton University

Percy Pike and his family
lived on a farm by the sea.

They spent all day working
in their tiny field.

But there was never enough to eat.

Early one morning, Percy came up with a plan.

He took a
long branch,

some string
and a nail.

Then he put them
together and made...

a fishing rod.

"I'll catch some fish and surprise everyone," he thought.

Sardines for supper!

Percy rowed around the bay.

He put a worm on his hook
and started to fish.

Percy waited... and waited...
and waited... He got so tired
of waiting, he fell asleep.

Hours later, he woke up – with wet feet.

Percy's boat was so old, it had sprung a leak.

Percy was sinking fast. Just
then, he saw a ship. "Help!"
he yelled.

I'm sinking!

The ship came closer.
"Please hurry!" he shouted.
Soon it would be too late.

At last, the ship came
alongside Percy's boat.

Take this
rope, lad!

Percy grabbed a rope and
pulled himself up.

With a big grin, he climbed
on board.

What luck!

Glug!
Glug!
Glug!

Percy saw who had rescued
him. Suddenly, he didn't feel
so lucky.

"I'm Captain Crook," growled a fierce man. "And this is my pirate ship."

My name's P-P-Percy Pike.

"Um, thanks for saving me," said Percy nervously.

"You have a choice, boy," boomed the captain. "Join my crew or...."

"I'll throw you to the sharks."

Percy didn't want to be a pirate. But he didn't want to be a shark's dinner, either.

"Tell Percy the ship's motto, lads," bellowed Crook, and the pirates sang.

We steal for Crook 'cos he's the best ♪ ♪ Then put the treasure in his chest. ♪ ♪

The ship sailed out to sea.
"Will I ever see my family
again?" thought Percy.

The next day, the pirates
spotted a ship called The
Crimson Cuttlefish.

Ship ahoy!

"Lead the attack, Sam!"
ordered Captain Crook.

18

Sam Scurvy
swung across
to the ship...

chased its crew...

and brought
back two
bags of shiny
gold coins.

19

"Put it all in my treasure chest," ordered the captain. Percy opened the chest.

Sam poured in all the gold. Well, almost all...

That night, Captain Crook looked in Sam's locker. He found twenty gold coins.

"Remember the ship's motto," roared the captain.

The next day, Crook made
Sam Scurvy walk the plank.
Sam jumped into the sea...

and was gobbled
up by sharks.

On Tuesday, the pirates
spotted a ship called The
Pink Prawn.

"Lead the attack, Willy!"
ordered Captain Crook.

Willy swung
across to the ship...

chased its
crew...

and brought
back a bag
of sparkling
diamonds.

24

"Put it all in my treasure chest," ordered the captain. Percy opened the chest.

Willy poured in all the diamonds. Well, almost all...

That night, Captain Crook
looked under Willy's bed. He
found thirty diamonds.

"Remember the ship's
motto," boomed the captain.

The next day, Crook made
Willy Weevil walk the plank.
Willy jumped into the sea...

and was gobbled
up by sharks.

On Thursday, the pirates spotted a ship called The Blue Blowfish.

Ship ahoy!

"Lead the attack, Ronnie!" ordered Captain Crook.

Ronnie Rum swung across to the ship...

chased its crew...

and brought back five bags of shiny silver coins.

"Put it all in my treasure
chest," ordered the captain.
Percy opened the chest.

Ronnie poured in all the
silver. Well, almost all...

30

That night, Captain Crook looked in Ronnie's spare boots. He found forty silver coins.

"Remember the ship's motto," roared the captain.

The next day, Crook made
Ronnie walk the plank.
Ronnie jumped into the sea...

and was gobbled
up by sharks.

That night, the captain spotted a ship called The Red Herring.

You're the last of my crew, lad.

"We're going aboard," said Captain Crook. "I'll keep watch. You look for treasure."

"And no tricks," he warned.
"Or else."

Gulp!

Percy and the captain
swung across to the ship. The
crew was fast asleep.

"Search the captain's cabin," barked Crook. "And don't come out empty-handed."

But Percy could only find maps. They gave him an idea.

Percy found a map of a place called Crab Island.

He took a pen and drew on the map. First, he drew a wiggly arrow.

Then he drew a big cross
by a waterfall.

Under the cross he wrote
the word treasure.

He left the cabin and took
the map to Captain Crook.

"I've found a treasure map," cried Percy with a smile.

"I'll be rich," chuckled Crook. "Back to my ship!"

The greedy captain couldn't
wait to find the treasure.
They sailed all night.

The next morning, they
landed on Crab Island.

The captain and Percy set off. They followed the wiggly line on the map...

across the beach,

around the lake,

between the rocks,

over the river,

until they reached the waterfall.

"Let me at that treasure," cried Crook, grabbing the shovel. He dug down

and down

and down

and down.

But the captain couldn't find any treasure.

There's nothing here.

Percy laughed. "I made it all up."

43

The captain turned red with rage. He tried to climb out of the hole, but he couldn't.

He was trapped.

"Help," yelled Crook.

But Percy wasn't listening.

Percy ran over the river,
between the rocks, around
the lake, across the beach
and back to the ship.

Percy took down the pirates' flag and set sail. Five days later, he arrived home.

There in the port were all the ships that Crook had attacked, so Percy returned their treasure.

Everyone was so grateful,
they gave Percy a big reward.

And the Pike family was
never hungry again.

Series editor:
Lesley Sims

First published in 2007 by Usborne Publishing Ltd., Usborne House, 83-85 Saffron Hill, London EC1N 8RT, England. www.usborne.com
Copyright © 2007 Usborne Publishing Ltd.